M000310124

Pukunui is a small Maori boy who lived 700 years ago, in Aotearoa (New Zealand).

This is his story...

To Nan and Pop.

First published 1976 by William Heinemann Ltd.
Auckland, Melbourne, London

This edition (2009) published by FireHydrant Creative Studios, Inc.
St. Louis, Mo. USA.
www.firehydrantcs.com

This book is copyrighted. Except for the purposes of fair reviewing, no part of this publication may be reproduced or transmitted in any form or by any means, electronic or mechanical, including photocopying, recording, or any information storage and retrieval system, without permission in writing from the publisher. Infringers of copyright render themselves liable to prosecution.

Text and illustrations © 1976 James Waerea.
Illustrations © 2009 James Waerea and Mitch Waerea.
The author asserts his moral rights in the work.

ISBN 978-0-9826066-0-5
Printed in the United States.

www.worldofpukunui.com

www.firehydrantcs.com

PUKUNUI

Words by James Waerea
Pictures by James and Mitch Waerea

A long, long, l-o-o-o-n-n-g time ago there was a small
Maori boy called Pukunui.
He lived in Aotearoa - 'The Land of the Long White Cloud.'

People called him Pukunui because he had such a big tummy.

His tummy was so big because he just loved to eat and eat and eat and eat.

Pukunui's home was in a Pa
which was on top of a hill,
right by the sea.

Every day when the tide had gone out,
he would go down to the seashore,
to gather seafood for his family.
"The seafood is good," said Pukunui.

Kapai te Kaimoana.

"Well done, Pukunui," said his father
when he returned to the Pa.
"When you are much bigger,
I will take you fishing in our canoe."

"But I am much bigger now," said Pukunui, trying hard to pull in his tummy and puff up his chest.
"There are many things to learn about the sea," his father replied.
"The sea can be very dangerous. But the day will come when you will be big enough to go fishing."

Pukunui was sad. Slowly he walked away. He didn't even want to eat his breakfast.

Shielding his eyes from the strong morning sun,
Pukunui stood on a rock and looked far out
across the big wide ocean.
Suddenly, he spotted a large school of fish
dancing across the waves.

Pukunui was excited. Climbing off the rock,
he rushed to where the canoe was lying in the sand.
He tied a flax rope around the prow of the canoe
and tried to drag it into the water.
But it was too heavy for him.

Nearby was a log. He rolled it into the water and took a paddle and a net from the canoe. Paddling away, he set off to where he had seen the school of fish.

He sang happily to himself...

"Hoea te waka..."

"Row the canoe..."

All of a sudden, without warning, a dark cloud appeared and burst open. Heavy rain pelted down.
The sky was growing black. Pukunui was frightened.

He threw the net over himself as protection against
the rain.
Pukunui gripped the paddle tightly. The waves were
getting bigger and bigger.

Huge waves tossed Pukunui up and down.
Each time he hit the water he paddled as fast as he could.
He knew that he couldn't stay on the log for very much longer.

Wooooommph!! Caaarash!!
Pukunui was thrown high into the sky, losing his paddle
and his net.

As quickly as the storm had started... it ended.
The sea was calm again. The rain had gone.
The sun had crept out from behind the clouds.
Pukunui found the log and clung to it, feeling very,
very tired.

It was dark when he finally drifted back to shore.
At the entrance to the Pa, he stopped.
He knew his father would be angry with him.
He peered inside.

As soon as his family and relations saw him,
they shouted with joy.
"Welcome Pukunui!" they cried,
"Look, Pukunui is safe!"
"Come Pukunui," his father called,
"we have been looking everywhere for you."

19 Tekau ma iwa

"Where have you been my son? We have been very worried."
"I have been fishing. I paddled out to sea on a log because
I wanted to catch plenty of fish for our people.
But there was a big storm."
His father looked at him and smiled.

"Sit down and eat. You must be very hungry,"
his father said.

"Tomorrow I will tell you about the sea and maybe we will
even go fishing."

Pukunui was happy again.

"The food is good," said Pukunui as he ate and ate and ate.

Maori Words to English

Pg.	Word	Meaning	Say
2	Pukunui	big tummy	Pook-koo-noo—ee
	Aotearoa/ New Zealand	the land of the long white cloud	Ao-tea-roa
4	kapai te kai	food is good	kaa-pie, teh, khy
5	Pa	village	Paa
6	kapai te kaimoana	seafood is good	kaa-pie, teh, khy-mor-aanah
12	Hoea te waka	paddle the canoe	Hoy-ah, teh, waa-kah
	Haere mai	welcome	Hy-reh, my
	Naumai	welcome	no-my
20	I hea koe?	Where were you?	ee, heh-a, kor-eh
24	tai tama e	young man	tie, tah-mah, eh
	Kia piki ai ki runga	so that it will climb on top (of the waves)	Kee-ah, pee-kee, eye, kee, rooh-nga

Numbers in English and Maori

1	Tahi		16	Tekau ma ono
2	Rua		17	Tekau ma whitu
3	Toru		18	Tekau ma waru
4	Wha		19	Tekau ma iwa
5	Rima		20	Rua tekau
6	Ono		21	Rua tekau ma tahi
7	Whitu		22	Rua tekau ma rua
8	Waru		23	Rua tekau ma toru
9	Iwa		24	Rua tekau ma wha
10	Tekau		25	Rua tekau ma rima
11	Tekau ma tahi		26	Rua tekau ma ono
12	Tekau ma rua		27	Rua tekau ma whitu
13	Tekau ma toru		28	Rua tekau ma waru
14	Tekau ma wha		29	Rua tekau ma iwa
15	Tekau ma rima		30	Toru tekau

23 Rua tekau ma toru

Hoea te Waka

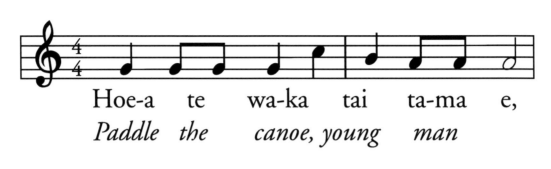

Hoe-a   te   wa-ka   tai   ta-ma   e,
Paddle   the   canoe, young   man

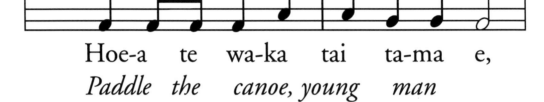

Hoe-a   te   wa-ka   tai   ta-ma   e,
Paddle   the   canoe, young   man

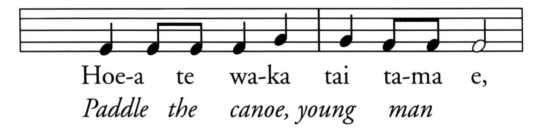

Hoe-a   te   wa-ka   tai   ta-ma   e,
Paddle   the   canoe, young   man

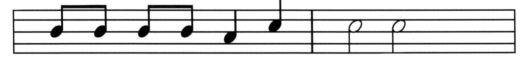

Ki-a   pi-ki   ai   ki   ru-nga,
so that it will climb on top (of the waves)

Ki-a   pi-ki   ai   ki   ru-nga.
so that it will climb on top (of the waves)

Next Book in the Series, Pukunui and his Friend Moata Moa.

About the Author

James Matariki Waerea, of Maori descent, is a native of Aotearoa/New Zealand. Waerea, a former school teacher, radio broadcaster, TV presenter, newspaper columnist and political cartoonist, wrote and illustrated his first children's book in 1962 while teaching. After having the book rejected many times by publishers because it contained Maori dialogue, it was not until 1978 that the first Pukunui book reached the marketplace. Four books have been published and in this current printing, his son Mitch helped with the illustrations. Mitch lives in Dallas, Texas, USA.

Visit Pukunui and his friends at

www.worldofpukunui.com

CPSIA information can be obtained
at www.ICGtesting.com
Printed in the USA
276210LV00006B

9 780982 606605

And Baby Makes 4

Written by Judith Benjamin

Graphics by Judith Freeman

Copyright © by Judith Benjamin, 2009

All rights reserved.

ISBN - 978-0-615-31682-6

No part of this book may be reproduced, stored in a retrieval system, or transmitted in any form or by any means – electronic, mechanical, digital, photocopy, recording – except for brief quotations for teaching, discussions, reviews and articles, without written permission of the author.

Motek Press

Printed in the United States of America

For my darling granddaughters
with love, from Nona.

And for Mark, My Love

Mama, Mommy and I are a family, just us three. We are like The Three Bears: Our family is *j-u-u-st* right!

But Mommy tells me something is changing. And it is ***Very Important!***

I am going to be a big sister! Mama is pregnant.
That means a baby is growing inside her!

Sometimes Mama tells me to come quickly. She puts my hand on her belly and I can feel the baby move.

I put my mouth close to Mama's belly. "Hi baby!" I shout. "I am your big sister. See you soon!"

I go to the doctor with Mama. I hear the baby's heart beating, and I can see what the baby looks like inside Mama.

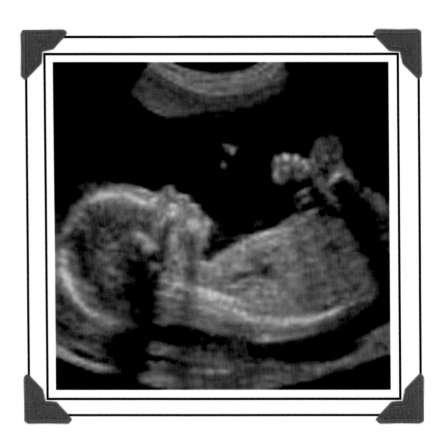

It doesn't look much like a baby, but Mama tells me it will when it is born.

People ask me if I will be getting a brother or a sister. But we don't know.

I answer, "It's a surprise!"

Mama tells me the new baby won't be able to play with me right away.

Mommy says the baby will cry a lot because that's the only way babies can say they need something.

Here is what new babies can do:
cry,
  suck,
    sleep,
      burp,
        hiccup,
          pee and poop.
And that is all until they get a little bigger.

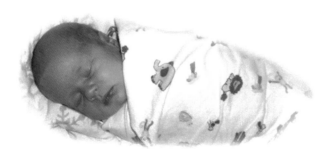

Sometimes Mama and I look at my baby pictures.
I couldn't do much either when I was very small.

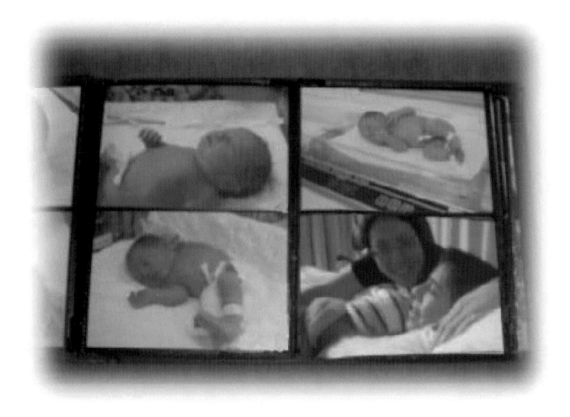

It is time for the baby to be born! Grammy comes and stays with me when my Moms go to the hospital. Grammy and I have fun while we wait. We make a cherry pie. No baby yet! Then we make cookies.

We wonder: Will the baby be a boy or a girl?

And guess what?

It's a BOY! I have a baby brother! They bring home our new baby. Now we have **four** in our family. I am a big sister!

Mama says, "We've decided to call him Jacob."

I think about that. Then I say, "I think I'll call him Jacob too."

And we do.

I told the children in my class about our new baby. Christopher asked, "Where is your daddy? And where is Jacob's daddy?" My teacher answered that lots of families are different from his. He has a Mommy and a Daddy. Some families have one parent, some have two Dads, some have two Moms like I have. There are other kinds of families too.

Here are some funny things about Jacob:

He has no tears when he cries. (Mommy said he will when he's a little bigger.)

He makes a lot of strange faces.

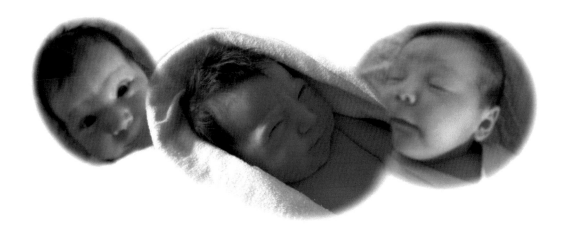

and strange noises--

Jacob's belly button looks like a boo-boo, but it's not. Mama said there used to be a cord there that brought him food when he was inside her. She said it's called an umbilical cord.

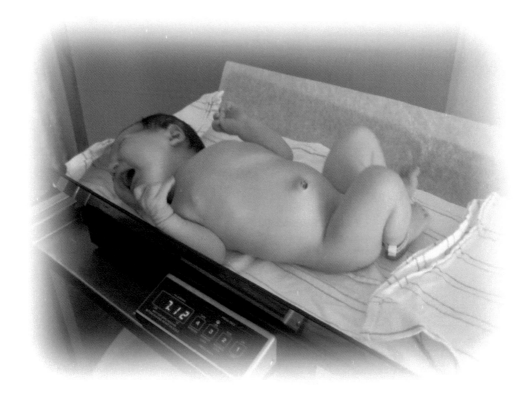

She said soon the piece of umbilical cord will drop off, and what's left will look like a real belly button.

I look at my belly button. I can't remember when mine looked like that. But a baby picture shows me it did.

Here are some things I don't like about baby Jacob:

He cries a lot.

w-a-a-a-h!!!

He wakes me up with all that loud crying.

One day he pulled my hair!

And Jacob gets way too many presents.

Mama and Mommy spend too much time with him.

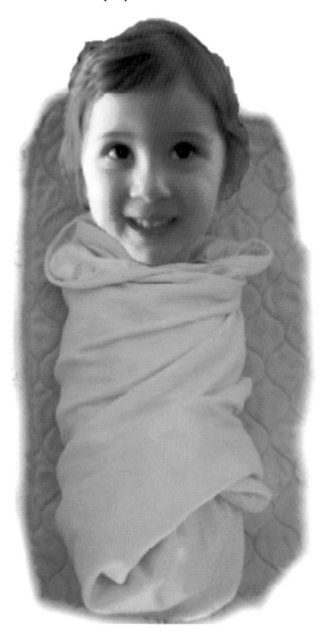

I WANT TO BE THE BABY!!

Sometimes I want to hurt that baby. My parents say I need to tell them about my feelings instead.

Sometimes I wish he would go away.

But here are some things I like about Jacob:

His fingers
      and toes

are so tiny and cute.

When I open his fist and put my finger in it, he grabs
my finger and holds on. I like it when he does that.

Sometimes my Mothers let me sit and hold him for a little while. One of them is always there to help.

Mama taught me something fun to do with Jacob. I bring my face near his and I slowly stick out my tongue. Sometimes he sticks his tongue out too!

Things I can do now to help with Jacob:

I bring clean diapers for him when he is getting changed.

Sometimes when Mama is changing his diaper, I talk in silly voices or sing and dance for him, and he listens. Mommy says he likes listening to my voice.

I have to be careful when he gets his diaper changed. One day he peed on me!

I help Mommy wrap him like a burrito in his blanket.
He likes feeling cozy.

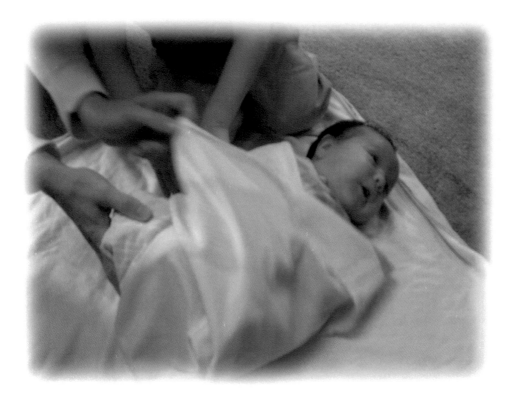

My Moms said Jacob will always look up to me because I am his big sister.

And you know what?

Now, having 4 in our family feels *j-u-u-u-st* right!

(You can paste a photo of yourself and the new
baby in your family here!)

CPSIA information can be obtained
at www.ICGtesting.com
Printed in the USA
276210LV00006B

9 780615 316826